D0127036

This book is based on the TV episode "Humbug," written by Scott Kraft, from the animated TV series *Miss Spider's Sunny Patch Friends* on Nick Jr., a Nelvana Limited/Absolute
Pictures Limited co-production in association with Callaway Arts & Entertainment, based on the Miss Spider books by David Kirk.

Nicholas Callaway, President and Publisher
Cathy Ferrara, Managing Editor and Production Director
Toshiya Masuda, Art Director • Nelson Gomez, Director of Digital Technology
Joya Rajadhyaksha, Associate Editor • Amy Cloud, Associate Editor
Raphael Shea, Senior Designer • Krupa Jhaveri, Designer
Bill Burg, Digital Artist • Christina Pagano, Digital Artist • Dominique Genereux, Digital Artist • Keith McMenamy, Digital Artist

Special thanks to the Nelvana staff, including Doug Murphy, Scott Dyer, Tracy Ewing, Pam Lehn,
Tonya Lindo, Mark Picard, Jane Sobol, Luis Lopez, Eric Pentz, and Georgina Robinson.

Library of Congress Cataloging-in-Publication Data available upon request.

Distributed in the United States by Viking Children's Books.

Visit Callaway Arts & Entertainment at www.callaway.com.

ISBN 0-448-44428-3

10 9 8 7 6 5 4 3 2 1 06 07 08 09 10

First edition, September 2006

Printed in China

"Your friends are here," Spindella laughed. "Get up, my love, and see!"
Spiderus gazed beyond his door. "They've really come for me?
The friends in dreams are fine," he smiled, "as long as you're asleep,
But ones you make when you're awake—those friends are yours to keep!"

But once again Spindella shook him out of his repose.
He wiped his bleary, teary eyes and honked his rosy nose.
"Oh what a happy place I've been," he coughed. "Too bad, it seems
That life awake can never be so sweet as in your dreams."

The grateful earwigs gathered 'round to thank their gracious friend—
A hero warm and generous, with eight strong hands to lend.
His hard, old heart was filled with pride. His eyes welled up with tears.
A hundred insects sang his praise. The village rang with cheers.

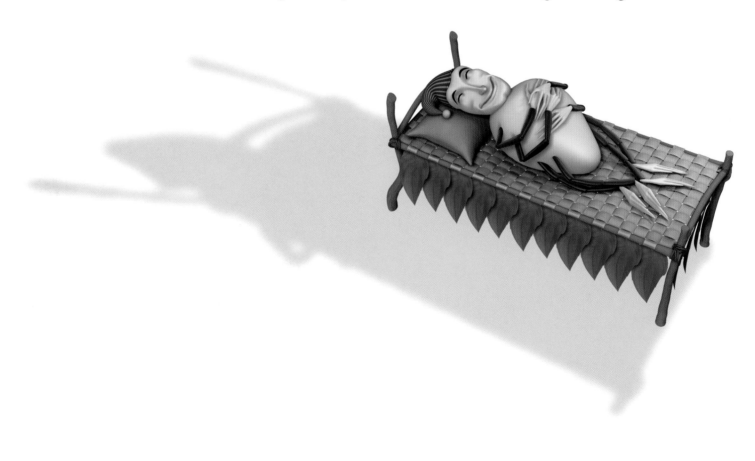

The deed was done. His spirits soared. Returning to his lair,
It wasn't long before sweet dreams were swirling through the air.
He drifted off to Slumberland. In just a little while
His grumpy sneer had disappeared—lips curled into a smile.

"Be still, my love, it's just a dream," Spindella whispered low.
"Then there's still time?" Spiderus gasped. "Stand back, I have to go!"
He loaded berries on his sleigh, and balanced even more,
Then piled them with a friendly note by Eunice Earwig's door.

Devouring fruit from every branch, he stuffed his bulging sack.
But as he gorged, the angry trees were grouping to attack.
They hurled their fruit like cannonballs. The snow was stained with red.
He tumbled down the hillside and woke screaming in his bed.

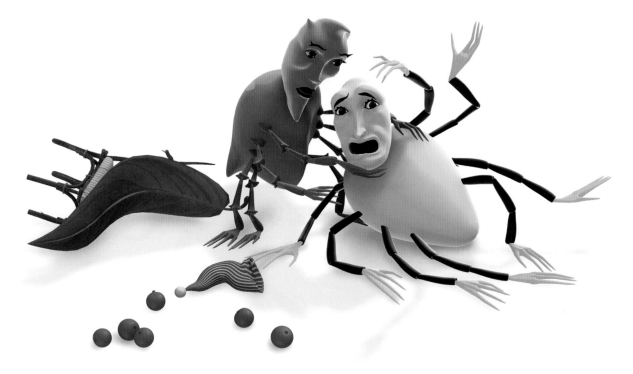

Spiderus, dozing by his fire, content, was dreaming, too,
Of nasty tricks that he had played and those he'd yet to do.
Like stealing food from little tykes—what joy to hear them whine.
He stuffed their berries in his mouth and laughed, "They're mine, all MINE!"

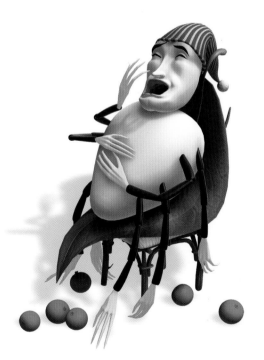

That night, in dreams, Bounce leapt through fruit, delicious, firm, and round,
While Shimmer soared among the starry clouds without a sound.
Wiggle dreamt he'd won a race. Holley saw an angel's face.
Everybuggy's dream revealed a glimpse of perfect grace.

"The dream bug, bah!" Spiderus growled. But then he changed his mind.
He cooed, "Dear boy, I'd like to help, if you would be so kind.
You've done your deed, now don't I need a dream bug visit, too?
Just drop this heavy burden. I'll deliver it for you."

"Don't eat me now, Spiderus, please! I'm doing my good deed.
Collecting yummy berry snacks—the earwigs are in need!
The dream bug's coming," Bounce explained. "I need to run, you see.
If I don't get my good deed done, there'll be no dreams for me."

So out among the snowy fields Bounce trudged behind his cart.
A heap of berries towered high as gladness filled his heart.
Spiderus, creeping from his lair, beheld the tender treat.
"How fortunate!" he bellowed. "You're in time for me to eat!"

Poor Bounce ran to his mother and explained his dismal plight.
"I need to do a deed that's good, and do it by tonight!"
Miss Spider smiled, "Dear Eunice sprained a pincer yesterday.
Why don't you gather winter food and take it up her way?"

The little bugs of Sunny Patch were studying the sky.
"We've all done our good deeds," said Squirt. "She wouldn't pass us by!"
"I've been a nice bug," Bounce exclaimed, "polite and kind and stuff—
As good as I could be. Oh no! . . . But was I good enough?"

With just a curl of frosty breath—a whisper barely heard,
She fills your head with lovely dreams, then sails without a word
To lace her graceful, golden thread in patterns through the night
Over, under, weaving wonder, winging out of sight.

Beneath the veil of shining stars, where insect angels dwell,
The dream bug glides with moonlit wings upon a cloudy swell.
Each solstice eve, she brings the joy that dreamers long to know,
And sows her seeds of goodness where they're likeliest to grow.